Talkaty Talker

Limericks by Molly Manley

illustrated by
Janet Marshall

Boyds Mills Press

Published by Bell Books
Boyds Mills Press, Inc.
A Highlights Company
815 Church Street
Honesdale, Pennsylvania 18431
Printed in Mexico

Publisher Cataloging-in-Publication Data
Marshall, Janet.
Talkaty talker : and other limericks / written by Molly Manley ;
illustrated by Janet Marshall.—1st ed.
(32)p. : col. ill. ; cm.
Summary: A collection of eleven limericks featuring brightly colored animals of all shapes and sizes.
ISBN 1-56397-195-X
1. Limericks, Juvenile. 2. Nonsense verses—Juvenile literature.
(1. Limericks. 2. Nonsense verses.) I. Marshall, Janet, ill. II. Title.
811.54—dc20   1994
Library of Congress Catalog Card Number: 92-75858

First edition, 1994
Book designed by Janet Marshall
The text of this book is set in 23-point Avant Garde.
The illustrations are done in cut paper.
Distributed by St. Martin's Press
Reinforced trade edition

10 9 8 7 6 5 4 3 2 1

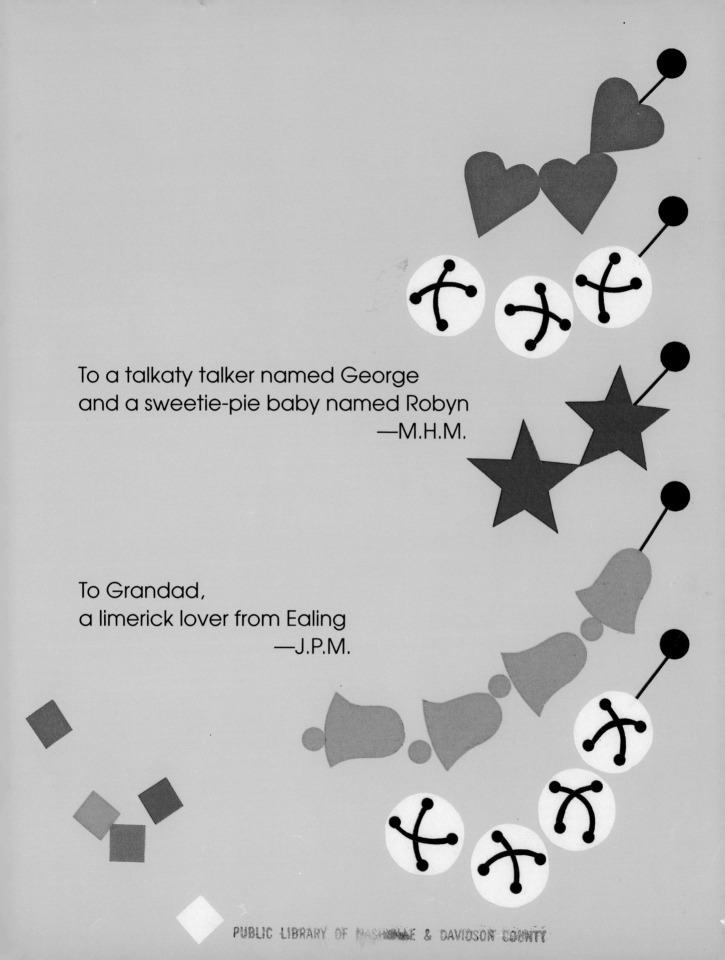

To a talkaty talker named George
and a sweetie-pie baby named Robyn
                    —M.H.M.

To Grandad,
a limerick lover from Ealing
                    —J.P.M.

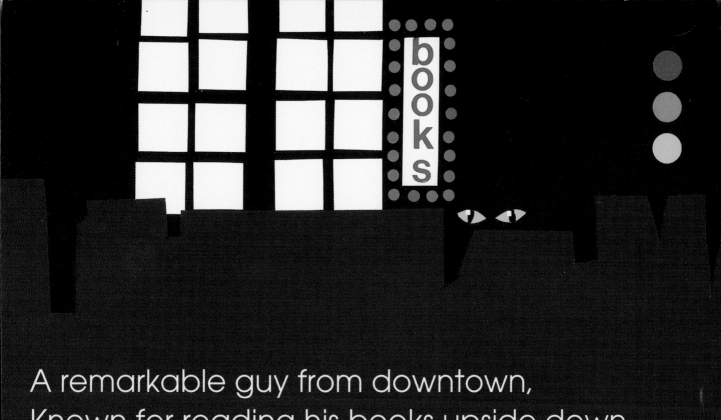

A remarkable guy from downtown,
Known for reading his books upside down,
Chose to stand on his head
In his bed while he read
And developed a permanent frown.

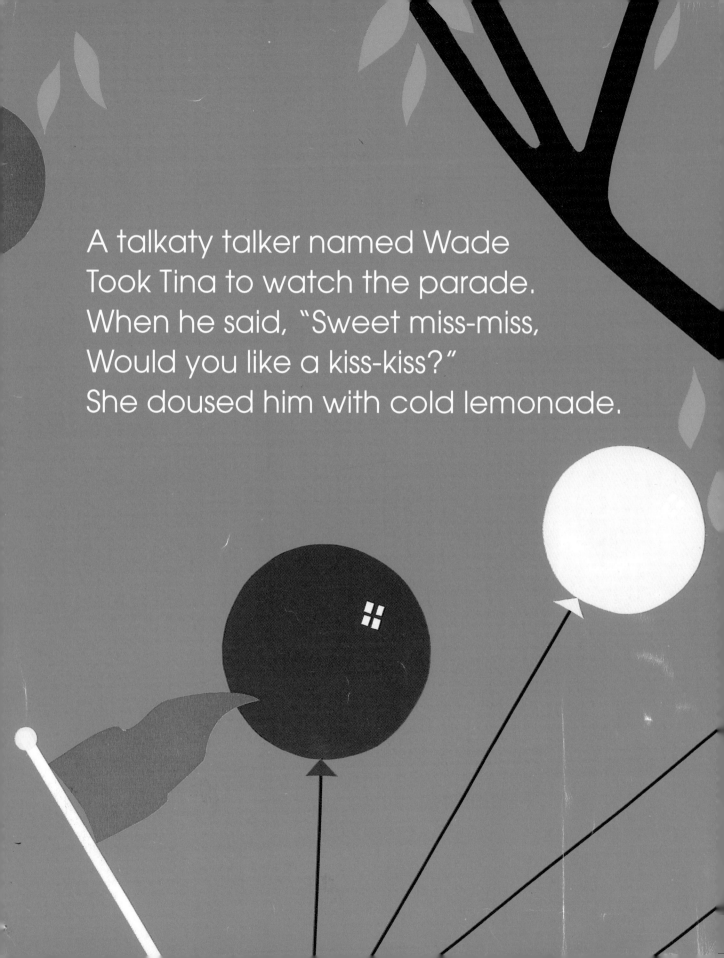

A talkaty talker named Wade
Took Tina to watch the parade.
When he said, "Sweet miss-miss,
Would you like a kiss-kiss?"
She doused him with cold lemonade.

A hot-air balloonist named Betty
Flew over a sea of spaghetti.
It looked quite suspicious,
But tasted delicious
With Parmesan cheese and confetti.

There once was an artist named Nellie,
Who painted her cottage with jelly,
And then on one shutter
She spread peanut butter
And slid down the stairs on her belly.

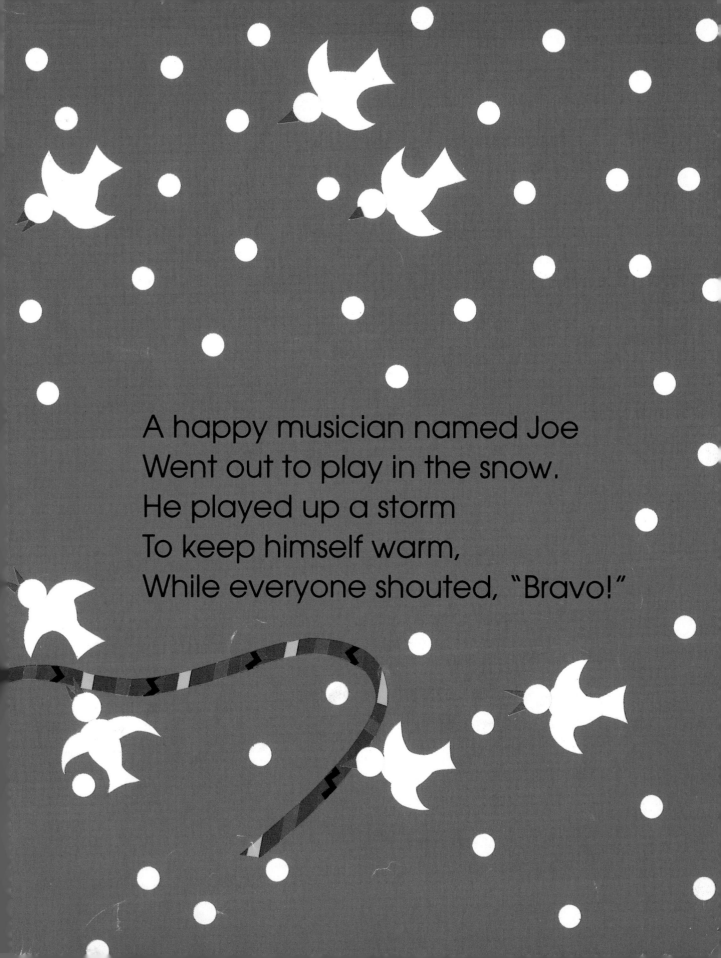

A happy musician named Joe
Went out to play in the snow.
He played up a storm
To keep himself warm,
While everyone shouted, "Bravo!"

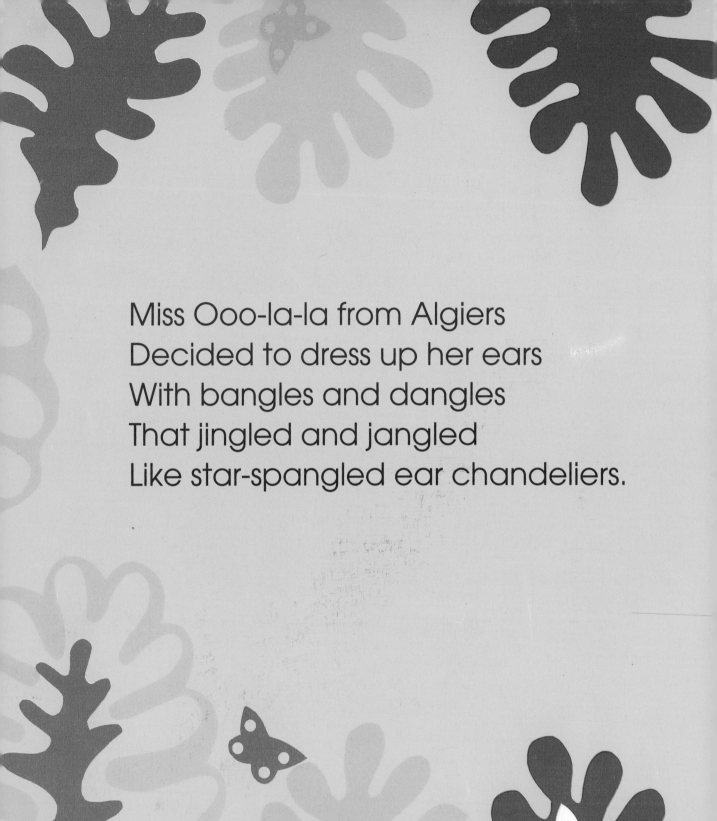

Miss Ooo-la-la from Algiers
Decided to dress up her ears
With bangles and dangles
That jingled and jangled
Like star-spangled ear chandeliers.

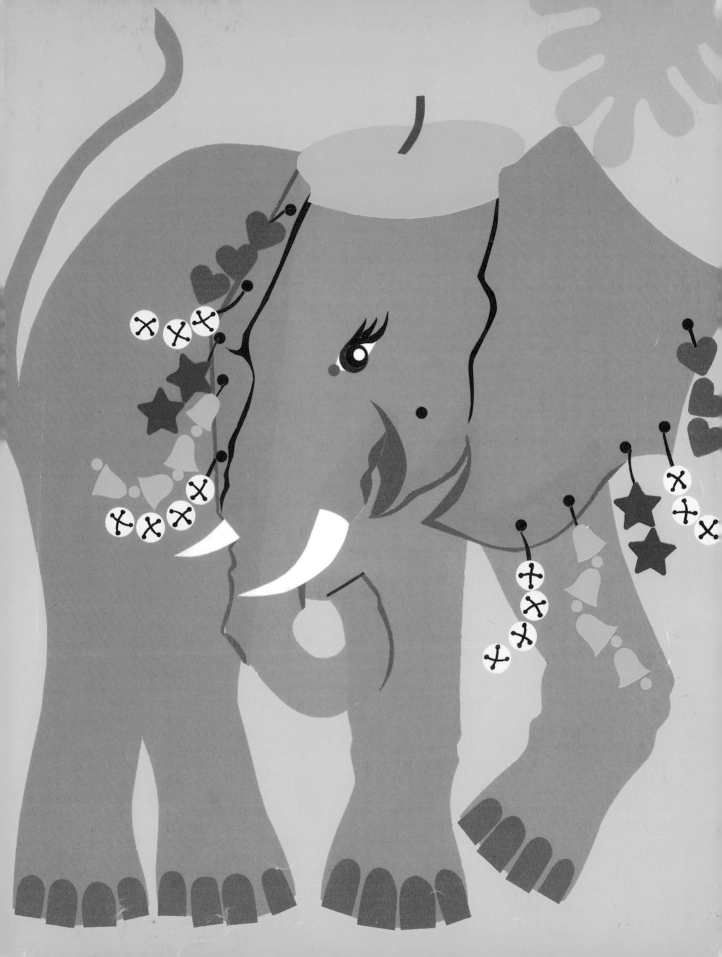

A two-year-old terror named Martie
Had a wonderful time at the party.
She threw her ice cream,
Made all the kids scream—
And that was the end of the party!

A young trick-or-treater named Bertie
Never washed and preferred to be dirty.
Then one Halloween,
He scrubbed his face clean,
And nobody knew he was Bertie.

Sally Lightfoot vacationed one day
On a reef down in Cane Garden Bay.
She thought it quite neat
To pinch passing feet
And scare all the swimmers away.

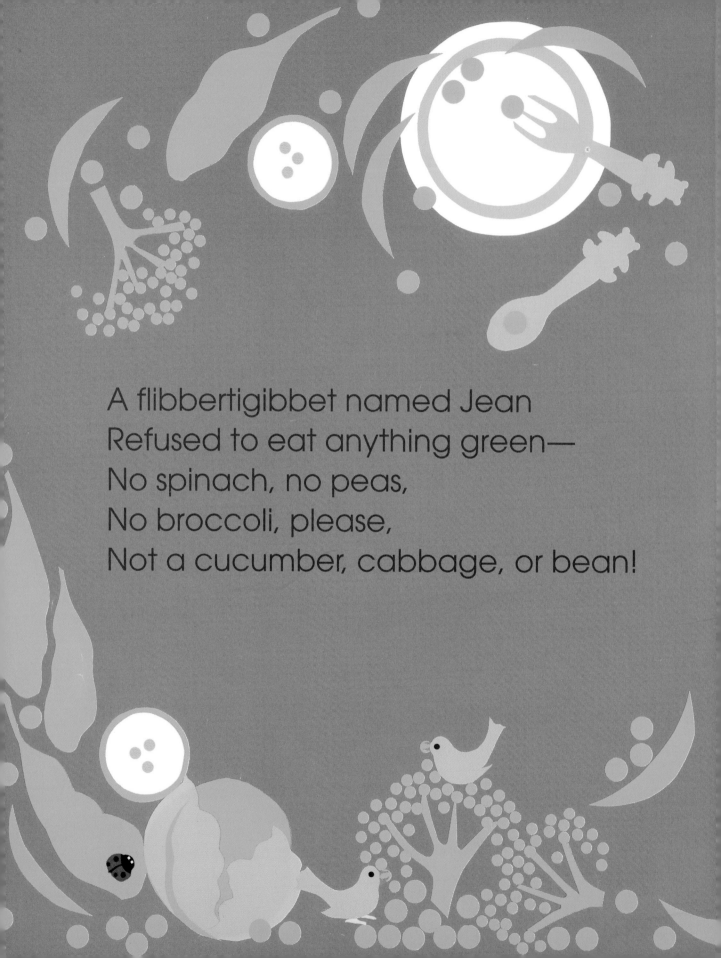

A flibbertigibbet named Jean
Refused to eat anything green—
No spinach, no peas,
No broccoli, please,
Not a cucumber, cabbage, or bean!

A sleepy-time baby named Pammie
Loves to sleep over with Grammie,
Who bakes apple pies,
And sings lullabies,
And rocks her to sleep in her jammies.

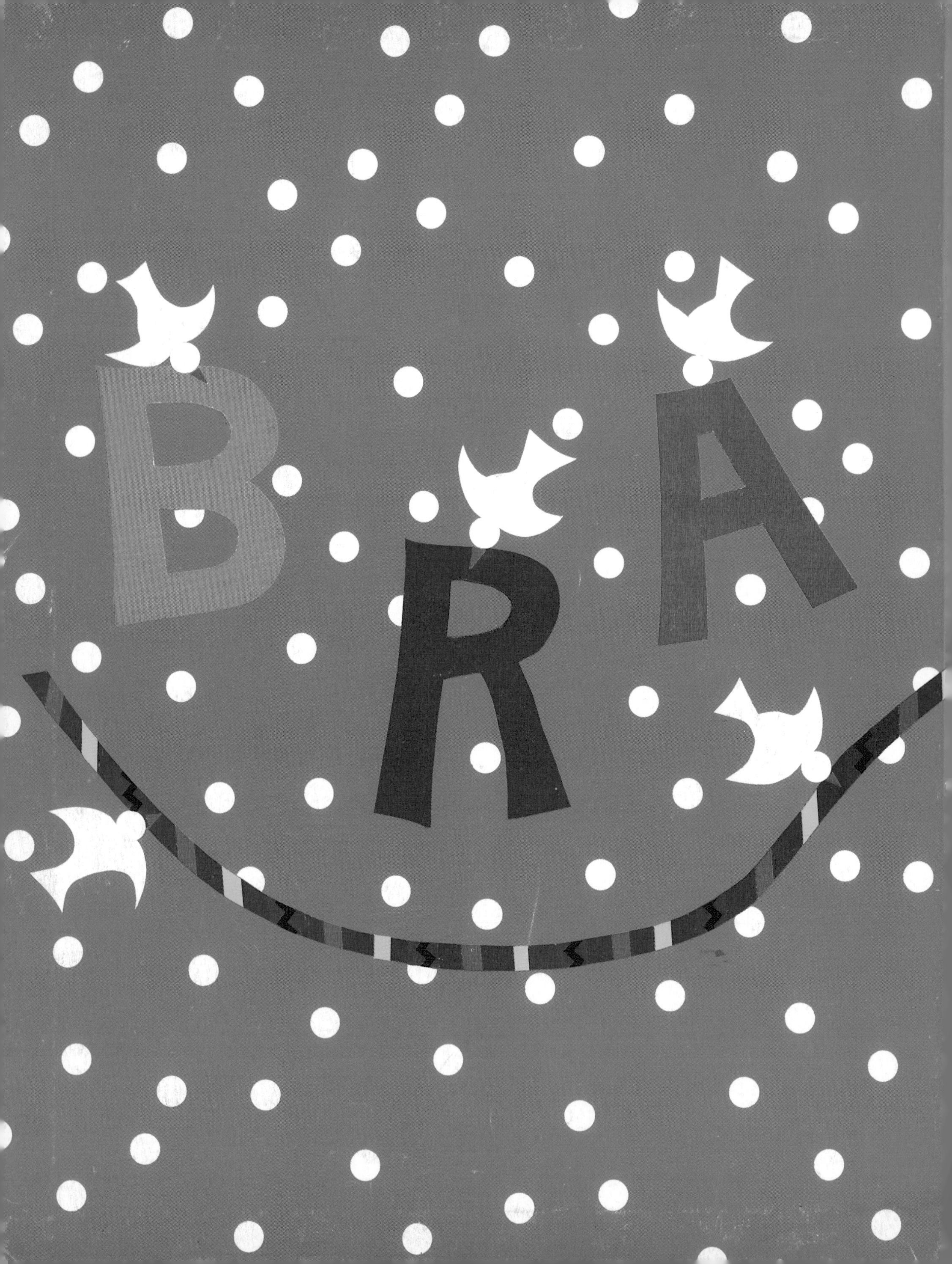
B
R
A